Clifford's
Best Pals

Elizabeth

This book
belongs

For Ben Liyanage

The author thanks Grace Maccarone
for her contribution to this book.

Copyright © 1985 by Norman Bridwell.

ISBN 978-0-545-22315-7

12 11 10 9 8 7 6 5 4   12 13 14

Printed in the U.S.A.   40
This edition first printing, May 2010

SCHOLASTIC READER
LEVEL 1
50-250 WORDS

Clifford's
Best Pals

Norman Bridwell

Cartwheel
·B·O·O·K·S· ®

SCHOLASTIC INC.
New York   Toronto   London   Auckland
Sydney   Mexico City   New Delhi   Hong Kong

Clifford has many pals.

Every day, they take a walk
around our town.

Today they see something interesting.

A ball swings from a truck.
Clifford wants to play with it.

That is not a good thing to do.
The dogs keep walking.

A can of red paint is about to spill
on a little white-and-brown dog.
"Look out!" says the painter.

Now the painter sees a big red dog.

"Was that magic paint?" he wonders.

Clifford sees three dogs playing in a pit.

Oh, no! They will be buried!

Clifford pushes the truck away.

He tries to help the men clean up.
Yuck!
Now Clifford needs a drink of water.

Someone turns on the hose.

Oh, no!

Next, Clifford's friends play on
a rocky hill.

Only Clifford sees the truck.

Clifford jumps up to stop it.

He pushes too hard.

Now Clifford's pals are having fun
in the big pipes.
Clifford wants to play, too.

But he is too big.

Clifford is stuck.
He can't see.

When Clifford falls down,
the pipe breaks off.

The workers can't do their jobs
with the dogs in the way.
They put Clifford's pals in a pen.

Clifford sees them stuck there.

He helps them get out.

The workers don't like that.
They trap Clifford in a net.

"This is not a good place for dogs to play," the workers say. "We need to do our jobs. We will let you go when we are done."

Clifford does not know what to do.
His pals chew the ropes to set
him free!

Now Clifford and his friends will find
a fun **and** safe place to play.